First American Edition 2017
Kane Miller, A Division of EDC Publishing

Page copyright © Kingsley Daley 2017
Illustrations copyright © Sav Akyüz 2017
The moral rights of the author and illustrator
have been asserted.

Hip and Hop, You Can Do Anything was originally published
in English in 2017. This edition is published by arrangement
with Oxford University Press.

For information contact:
Kane Miller, A Division of EDC Publishing
PO Box 470663
Tulsa, OK 74147-0663
www.kanemiller.com
Library of Congress Control Number: 2017932949

Printed in China
1 2 3 4 5 6 7 8 9 10
ISBN: 978-1-61067-683-0

Here's Blueberry Hill – Hip and Hop's endz.
Where they go to school and play with friends.
Hop loves to dance. Hip loves to rhyme.
Come and join them. It's Hip and Hop time.

All the children are getting ready for the Blueberry Hill bike race.

Hip is riding FAAAAASSST!

The Cheeky Monkeys are doing AWESOME stunts.

Hop is not having fun.
He dreams of racing his bike,
but he doesn't know how to ride.

"I don't think I can do it," he says.

"You CAN do it," says Hip. "You have to follow your dreams and practice."

"You can do anything if you try,
You can do anything, ride or fly.
Don't let anybody tell you no.
Focus on your dreams and go!"

"Don't worry," say the Cheeky Monkeys.
"You just have to learn to balance.

"The Cheeky Monkeys are right," says Hip.

"You can do anything if you try,
You can do anything, ride or fly.
Don't let anybody tell you no.
Focus on your dreams and go!"

"Don't worry," says Kofi. "You just have to learn to use your brakes.

"If you're moving too fast, don't panic.
Use your brakes well, it's the best habit.

Just slow down and take your time.
Practice hard and you'll be fine."

"Kofi is right," says Hip.

"You can do anything if you try,
You can do anything, ride or fly.
Don't let anybody tell you no.
Focus on your dreams and go!"

CRASH!

And before anyone
can say another word . . .

Hop flies off to sit in a tree.

"Little birds can't ride bikes," he says.

"Little birds should stick to flying!"

"Listen up," says Hip.

"I'm going to tell you a story about a little bird I once knew.

"There was a little bird who was a trailblazer.
He learned so much that it would amaze ya.

He learned to write. He learned to talk.
He learned to fly before he could walk.

He inspires me because
he's smart and kind.

**The coolest bird you
could ever find.**

"That little bird is you," says Hip.

"You learned to do all of those amazing things—and you can learn to ride, too."

"You're right," says Hop. "Little birds never give up!

"We're all beginners when something's new.
Now look at everything we can do.
I would never have learned to fly,
If I'd just given up and refused to try."

Hop practices . . .

and practices . . .

. . . and practices.

Soon it is the day of the Blueberry Hill bike race.
Everyone cheers as the children
ride past.

Hip is riding FAAAAASSST!

The Cheeky Monkeys are doing AMESOME stunts.

Kofi is riding HIGH . . .

And a little bird comes riding too.

Past Hip,

past the Cheeky Monkeys,

Everyone cheers for Hop—
the little bird who never gives up!

And they all say together:

"You can do anything if you try.
You can do anything, ride or fly.
Don't let anybody tell you no.
Focus on your dreams and go!

Practice, practice and you'll be a winner.
Every expert starts as a beginner.
Drawing, dancing, or playing the drums,
With a whole lot of practice you'll be the one.

You can do anything if you try.
You can do anything, ride or fly.
Don't let anybody tell you no.
Focus on your dreams and go!"

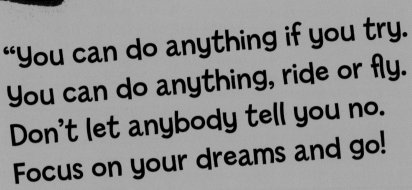

WHAT DREAMS WILL YOU FOLLOW?